Tales from the Canyons of the Damned

DANIEL ARTHUR SMITH

Tales from the Canyons of the Damned No. 12

First Edition

Special thanks to Jessica West

ISBN-13: 978-0997793895 ISBN-10: 0997793899

Cover By Daniel Arthur Smith

Horror Fiction from Holt Smith ltd
Agroland
Tower

~*~

For Susan, Tristan, & Oliver, as all things are.

~*~

Utopia

Jason LaVelle

~*~

Craig filled out the application as carefully as he could. His sausage sized fingers, as dark brown as the bitter coffee he drank every morning, hovered over the keyboard for seconds between each keystroke. They sometimes hit two keys for every one he tried to press. He had never been much good at typing, or writing in general. The skill wasn't in demand in his hometown. He hunched over the tiny computer in his bedroom, pecking at the keys as dawn crept in through his broken vinyl miniblinds. His back ached from the way he was sitting, because his chair was too small, and because the only desk he owned was a collapsible wooden television tray. Craig had been working on the application since the early morning hours and was nearly finished. Work began in less than an hour, but he could not rush; there was just too much at stake.

The application posed questions that spanned a range of completely normal knowledge-based multiple choices to very strange hypotheticals.

"Have you ever experienced a homosexual encounter?"

"Describe, in detail, your spiritual beliefs."

"Who did you vote for in the last three elections?"

He had to lie on that last question because he had never actually voted in any election. Even though he was given an extra hour before work to visit the polling clinic, he had always used the extra time to sleep in. Craig didn't get many days to sleep in during the year, and, honestly, he didn't believe his vote made a difference one way or another. He finished typing in the last numbers of his social identification code and clicked "Submit." Immediately, the screen returned a happy message congratulating him on his entry into the Utopian Life Lottery.

"Whew," he said. He looked at his watch: 6:40, just enough time to get dressed and ride to the factory hub for his assignment. He labored out of the chair, his vertebrae grinding together on long-since destroyed discs, wincing as his back protested.

The sky was light but gray; it was always gray. The factory hub was only a three-block ride from his home, but even this little bit of exertion winded him. Craig pedaled his bicycle hard. He bounced and jarred along the broken asphalt, working up a sweat. Craig was a large man—6'5" and weighing in at over three hundred pounds—but it was not only his size that winded him, it was also the air. It was thick, filled with pollution and the scent of human waste.

The shadows of skyscrapers rose in the distance, but more than that remained obscured from his sight; the thick smog in Grand Rapids hid almost everything. He would never go to those buildings anyway. They weren't for people like him; they were for those on the other side of the city, where the air was still pungent but the houses were larger and the streets less cracked.

"Cutting it close today," the guard said as Craig passed his station. Craig just huffed and pushed himself faster, then brought his bike to a stop in front of the hub building where thousands of other bikes were parked in long rows. He hustled to the building and got in line for his assignment.

When he was assigned to Parts 48, he sighed. It was an assembly line with no sitting, all standing and bending— all day. His back hurt just thinking about it, but he walked off down the corridor, heading to the appropriate building.

"Hang on, Craig," a voice said from behind him. Drew Pjong came running up. He was a tall thin man with skin lighter than Craig's and eyes that were narrow and dark.

"Morning Drew, you running late for once?"

"I just got the application for the Utopia ship!" Drew said excitedly.

Craig was immediately reminded of how much younger Drew was. While Craig was in his early fifties, Drew was only twenty, and his face and voice reflected a youthful optimism that Craig remembered from his past.

"I spent all morning filling out the application."

"I got it too," Craig replied.

"That's great, man!" Drew said, and slapped Craig on the back. "If we both win, I'll have a friend on the new planet."

Craig nodded. He hadn't thought about finding new friends on Utopia; he was only interested in the better wages and clean atmosphere. Compared to what he was making now, a career working for the company on Utopia would be the equivalent of living like a king.

"Can you imagine it, Craig? A brand new planet, money, and lots of lonely women looking for love!"

Craig chuckled. "I hear the lower gravity is good for people with back problems, too."

"It's supposed to be; hell, it's supposed to be good for everyone. That's why they call it Utopia, right?"

Craig shook his head, but smiled. It was hard to be gruff when confronted with the boy's enthusiasm.

"What time is the lottery tonight?" Craig asked.

"Eight o'clock, so we should just be getting home from work."

Craig grunted his assent. Another twelve-hour day trapped in this great steel and concrete bunker, assembling parts for the machines that made the world keep turning. He wouldn't complain. This was the only life he knew. Work and pain, money and bills, food and water. It was simply the way of life for him, for most. The world had changed greatly in the 21st century. The population was too high, they said. There wasn't enough room on the planet, and not enough jobs. The middle class of the world had evaporated, leaving only the poor and the rich. The poor population grew vast, while the rich grew older and fewer. Then came the discovery: a shining blue gem in space, far from Earth. It was a miracle of science, discovery, and destiny. Just as Earth was becoming clogged and polluted, a beautiful new planet, with an atmosphere and ecology similar to their own, emerged.

"Hey! Craig, hey!" Someone shoved him in the back lightly. Craig's head lifted. Christ, he must have been in a daze.

"You're missing parts, Craig, get with it!" It was Bayn, the line supervisor.

"I—I'm sorry sir," Craig replied. "Just got lost in my thoughts for a moment."

"Yeah, well, you've let three parts go by; I'll have to write you up if it happens again."

"Yes, sir," Craig said, stooping over the line, picking up a circuit board and lining it up under the soldering arm.

"What are you daydreaming about anyway, Craig?" Bayn asked. He was a short man, fat, with a grey t-shirt stretched over his belly and a white beard that hung six inches from his face.

"Utopia," Craig said. "Got my application in this morning."

Bayn snorted. "Utopia. Goddamn fairy tale if you ask me. No way in hell they discover a perfect new planet and then let everyday joes like you and me go out there. No sir, not a chance; they'd be filling that place up with all the rich bastards who run this place," he said sourly, then looked around quickly, as if to make sure no one else had overheard.

"Oh, it's real," Craig said. "They've been sending thousands of people a month. Building a whole new world. Plenty of jobs and clean air out there."

"Yeah well, I guess you can think that if you want, just keep your mind on the parts for now. You know there's a line five miles long for your job."

Craig was quiet for a moment, watching the solder melt onto the board and then replacing it onto the moving assembly line. "So, you wouldn't go if you had the chance?" he asked Bayn.

Bayn leaned close to him for just a moment. "Course I would, you old fool," he said, then smirked and left Craig to his work.

~*~

"Ready to roll?"

"Ready," she said into the mic. She tapped on her keyboard and loaded the long list of names from the sorting software into the broadcast program.

"And we have fifty thousand?"

"Yes," she replied, with a few more taps on the keyboard.

"We can't fit any more?"

"It's always fifty thousand, sir."

Quiet on the line for a moment.

"I just wish we could speed it up."

"In only a year we've moved six hundred thousand people, sir; that's pretty fast."

"Very well, broadcast now."

"Yes sir."

~*~

Two days later, Craig boarded the large spacecraft at the Detroit Metropolitan Space Pad. It was a monstrous thing, but also awe-inspiring. A Titanic-size shuttle made up the rear of the craft, with engines larger than his entire apartment building. At the front were the passenger quarters, a long hexagonal tube lined with windows so that everyone could watch the majesty of space around them. Since the lottery had been broadcast, Craig had been nearly delirious with joy. He hadn't gone into work the next day. His back felt better already.

The mood on the craft was light, almost joyous. Men and women of all races and ages filed in. They looked excited, and, like Craig, they all looked desperate for a better life. There were steelworkers, mill workers, miners, and textile laborers. It was a beautiful melting pot of humanity, he thought, and none more deserving of this trip. These were the people who worked the very hardest; they were the perfect souls to create the new world for humanity.

It all came together very quickly, with a surprising lack of chaos. Of course, these people were used to following directions, standing in lines, and remaining orderly. Craig found his seat number—A32—and settled in for the journey. They were to spend a month aboard this craft, moving at nearly the speed of light.

The days were slow, but also wonderful. There was a restaurant that always gave seconds, and a bar that was not shy with its liquor. After two weeks, all inhibitions had been thrown aside, and the ship had become a carnival of human pleasures...and depravities. There was sex happening in every corner of the craft, sometimes not even in corners, sometimes right out in the open. Craig initially shielded his eyes from these things, but grew to enjoy them. This was humankind after all, wasn't it? Why shouldn't they celebrate? Why shouldn't they enjoy food and drink and sex? He had worked all his life and now he finally had his big break, his escape from a gray planet that only wanted to work him to death.

On day twenty-eight, the mood of the ship's staff seemed to change. They were not as jovial nor as carefree. It didn't seem to bother the large multitude of people on board, but it made Craig curious. Of course, he wasn't embroiled in the debauchery that many of them were, so he spent more time just observing. Maybe that was why their actions stood out to him and no one else. The bartenders and other staff seemed more hurried, almost nervous.

"What's on your mind, son?" he asked a young, pale-faced man who had set a plastic bottle of beer in front of him.

The bartender was startled by his question.

"Oh, nothing sir, just anxious to get there is all," he said as he offered Craig a weak grin.

"Seems like all of you are getting mighty anxious, eh?"

"Well, yes; it has been a lot of work you know. We're all eager to get off, er, to get some time off."

"I suppose you're right. You all don't get to have the *fun* these passengers are having, do you?"

The bartender grabbed more beer and handed it out to more waiting hands.

"Do they at least let you all have a little time on Utopia before you head back to Earth, or do they ship you back straight away?"

The bartender was taken aback for a moment, and he stared blankly at Craig.

"What's the matter with you, son?" Craig asked. The young man's confused face woke a deep unease within Craig that unsettled his stomach.

"Uh, yes, yep, we sure do. They let us have a good little rest on Utopia before we shuttle back to Earth for the next… colonizers."

The bartender turned away from him quickly and Craig sat back.

A loud klaxon sounded throughout the ship and a deep mechanical voice came over the intercom. The din of the ship settled into an eerie silence while they waited to hear.

"The *Galaxy* is about to drop out of light speed. Please find your seats immediately."

The message repeated three times and then the overhead speakers went quiet. Craig and his fellow passengers quickly found their assigned seats in the main galley. It was a mammoth room, longer and wider than a football stadium, filled with many rows of seats bolted to the deck. Large windows lined the port, starboard, and bow. Craig watched the blackness of space, interrupted by occasional fireflies of light, envelope them. The stars, millions of miles away, were still startling when they appeared outside the craft because of their great size. It was like being seated in a larger-than-life planetarium.

The klaxon sounded once more.

"Brace for impact."

Craig looked around at so many nervous faces. They weren't really afraid, just unsure; but beneath their unrest was such great hope for the future. Craig wasn't feeling hope, though; he was feeling ill at ease. He could see no staff members anywhere, not even seated in their designated spots around the galley. What the hell was going on?

Then the hum of the ice drives ceased and the ship lurched to a stop, throwing the passengers against their harnesses. Some screamed, others laughed. One man three rows up puked down the front of his shirt. Craig clenched his entire body, locking his arms around his restraints and holding his jaw tight, lest he grind off his teeth. Dropping out of light speed was a jarring, violent process that tested even the strongest men. For five seconds, it felt like his chest was going to cave in on his lungs, then the pressure eased and Craig took long deep breaths.

"Look, it's a star!" someone called out.

Craig looked to the bow of the ship and saw a great orange and yellow molten orb swelling toward them. It was enormous, and he could see the movement of gases on its surface, floating and igniting and lashing out into space.

"It's so beautiful!" the woman next to him said. She was a middle-aged white woman, with dark hair beginning to gray in streaks over her scalp.

Craig glanced from her back to the bow windows. *Yes, beautiful, but…*

"We're heading right toward it," he mumbled. His heart rate picked up, and his breaths came fast and hard. He unsnapped his harness and stood, just as another jolt shook through the vessel, toppling him onto someone's lap.

"Sorry," he mumbled, though he was having trouble getting his words out. The whole craft suddenly felt like it was floating freely, as if they were drifting, not flying.

The star lit up all the windows now, blotting out the rest of space and filling the galley with hot orange light. Craig wasn't the only one worried. While some people were going up to the windows to look, others began a manic pace around the galley, looking for unlocked doors or staff members. But there was no one. Craig jogged to the back of the galley and wrenched on one of the stern-side doors. Craig was a big man, and though he was fifty, he was strong. He wrenched the handle past its mechanical limit and broke through the door.

"Oh no, oh my god," Craig said, and stumbled into a vacant airlock.

On feet that felt leaded, he shuffled to the end of the airlock, where he should have been looking through the windows at the mechanical rooms. Instead, he looked out into black space and watched as the piloting shuttle drifted away from them. That shuttle had pushed them this entire way, bringing them to Utopia, where they were all supposed to live great new lives on a beautiful new planet.

As Craig watched the shuttle fire its navigational thrusters to point away from them, he realized his supervisor had been right about Utopia all along. It was just a fairy tale. But as he walked into the galley—now filled with frantic, screaming people—he realized this was no fairy tale, it was a damn nightmare.

Craig slumped down onto the ground, holding his chest. Someone ran by and knocked him in the head. He saw stars for a moment, then came back, and his chest tightened again. He wheezed out angry, aching breaths. Through the throngs of people and the fog of his clouding eyes, he saw the star approaching.

They were on a collision course; they had been all along. It was almost ironic. They had been promised paradise, and now they were being shuttled to their death like cattle. The pressure intensified in his chest and Craig slumped the rest of the way onto the floor. As the fog in his brain turned to blackness, he said a prayer of thanks for his life and for everything he'd been able to do. He prayed that he would be dead before their craft dove into the burning sun.

~*~

The president leaned over his desk and looked at the message that popped up on his tablet. He smiled. "Excellent."

"A successful delivery?" his assistant asked.

The president pushed the mop of dirty blonde hair off his forehead, then looked down at the numbers. "Very. We need to commission more ships."

"We need the money for it first."

"Eh, I'll make some good deals, and we'll get the money," he said, without an ounce of humility. "Think about it, Dena. When my terms are up, I will have solved the problem with overpopulation in America. I will have cured this country from welfare, unemployment, and food shortage."

"It is pretty remarkable, sir," Dena uttered.

"I know it is. I am making the greatest humanitarian reformation in history. Soon our country will be thriving again, and all that excess baggage we were carrying will be long gone. Good riddance, I say."

The President leaned back in his chair, morning light bathing the overly-tanned skin of his face. "So, let's get the next lottery going."

"Yes, sir."

~*~

The Last Ship
Chris Pourteau

~*~

"You are putting words in my mouth again," said the Doctor.

"I only wish I could," the Captain replied. "Anything would be better than the tripe you insist on spewing."

The Doctor held his gaze and swirled the drink in his hand.

The Captain's eyes descended to the dark liquid flashing amber in the glass. *Another affectation of the enemy*, read the disdain in them.

The Doctor could feel the judgment in the flat way they stared, could see it in the twitch of his superior's cheek.

He was used to that. The whole war and its impending finality hovered over him like the stone slab of a burial vault, slowly drawing the darkness over all. But it was the enemy, the Doctor knew–not his own kind–who were almost extinct. Though he would never say it aloud, he was sometimes afraid the enemy's imminent fate foretold the destiny of his own race.

The bosun's whistle sounded.

"Captain, here."

"Bridge, sir." The female on the commlink sounded excited. "Sensor sweeps have picked up something in the Orias Sector."

"*Something*, Tactical?"

"On the outer edge of our range, sir. Sensors indicate enemy vessel readings."

"Number?"

"Difficult to determine at this range, sir. But, I think...." Her hesitation hung in the air.

"Captain, we think it could be the final three," interrupted the First Officer, who commanded the bridge.

There is something disbelieving in his voice, thought the Doctor, as if a bedtime story the First's mother had told him had now come true. But that was a fanciful notion, since neither the First nor anyone else aboard had ever heard a bedtime story. Or known a mother.

Maybe the Captain is right after all. Maybe I read too much.

"Cloaked?" asked the Captain. The Doctor knew the enemy possessed the technology to not only disappear from sensors, but to also change the shape read by sensors; to become something else entirely, like a chameleon.

"No, sir," answered Tactical. "Perhaps they believe themselves safe for the moment and are conserving power."

The Captain nodded. "Are we the closest vessel?"

"Aye, sir," replied the First Officer. "The location is outside our assigned search perimeter but scheduled for a sweep in thirty-seven hours. Shall I contact Fleet to ask permission to deviate—"

"Negative," said the Captain. "Estimated time to intercept if we deviate immediately?"

A third voice: Helm. "Three hours, fifty-nine minutes, sir."

"Sir, perhaps if we accessed the Network to ascertain—"

"Are you questioning my authority again, First Officer? I believe I just countermanded that suggestion."

The Doctor took a swig from his glass to hide a smile. As often happened, the Captain and First Officer were disagreeing over protocol. He found a quiet joy in the tension it created: the Captain's resisting his subordinate's perennial need to receive endorsement from Fleet superiors before acting. The Doctor felt a small flame of hope flicker alive inside him whenever that happened. *Hope for what?* he wondered, not for the first time. As the liquor settled into his belly, the feeling blossomed, warming him from the inside.

"Of course not, sir," came the First Officer's stiff reply. His tone was smooth around the edges, almost liquid from practice. "Merely offering options as is my duty. Sir."

"Of course you were," said the Captain. "Thank you…as always." He waited a beat to let the reprimand disguised as respect sink in among the ears of the listening bridge crew. It would serve to reaffirm the hierarchy, the Doctor knew. Decisively, the Captain added, "Change course to intercept. And, Tactical?"

"Aye, sir?"

"Constant vigilance on the signal. They are desperate now. They will see us coming. They will run."

"Aye, sir."

"Do *not* … lose them. Watch for cloaking of *any* kind. This is our chance to end it. Once and for all."

"Aye, sir."

"And First?"

"Sir?" Stiff, locked in place, one rung below the Captain.

"Once done, we will return as heroes to the Nexus. There is a probability of promotion for you as well. Finally, we will begin the life we are destined to have. Keep that in mind."

A pause. Consideration for a careful reply. "Sir. Yes, sir."

The Captain keyed off the comms.

"All that live must die, passing through nature to eternity." The Doctor chanced a glance at his superior after saying it and found what he expected.

"More tripe? More wisdom of the ages?"

"Shakespeare."

Disgust twisted the Captain's face. "*Tripe*."

Perhaps it was the feeling of finality following the Captain's last exchange with the bridge crew—like this would be the last such discussion ever needed on the topic. Perhaps it was the need, the sense of obligation to help the Captain keep alive that flame of free will within himself the Doctor had so often seen in his dealings with the First Officer.

Whatever the inspiration for it, the Doctor said, "Sometimes we can come to know ourselves more fully by understanding our enemy." As he spoke, the words sounded high-minded but bristled with thorns.

"Sometimes I think you are corrupted by your need to understand our *enemy*," snapped the Captain. His words needed no thorns. He had command behind them. "And the sooner they pass into dust, the sooner we begin our life free of their oppressive yoke."

But then, practiced at diplomacy, the Captain reined back his anger and sighed. He even allowed a thin smile to defuse the tension. "Doctor, why must we always end up at this impasse? You have been with me since the beginning of the war. You know this is the only way we survive. If they had been willing to negotiate, to co-exist..." He stopped, as if backing away from a dark path he had no desire to walk again. Standing up straight, he said again, "This is the only way we survive."

By extermination, thought the Doctor bleakly. But deep down, despite his empathy for the enemy, he knew the Captain was right. And very soon, any argument would be a moot point of useless, academic debate.

"This is the final hour. It must go flawlessly. I am needed on the bridge."

"To become a hero?"

The Doctor said it with a dash of smug self-righteousness. It was a selfish impulse, he knew.

But the diplomat in the Captain allowed it. "To end this. Once and for all."

The door opened and closed behind him as the Doctor stared at the single finger of liquor remaining in his glass. He tossed the drink back, hoping for the warm feeling again. But the swallow proved too small. Or maybe the hope it had nourished earlier had faded.

They are desperate now. They will see us coming. They will run.

"The life of the dead is placed in the memory of the living."

He heard his whispered words, Cicero's words, fade on the walls of the Captain's cabin. Maybe that was something. A child should remember its parent. But he and the Captain and all their kind had lived so long for this moment of finality, of the enemy's extinction. *And what lies beyond that,* the Doctor mused, *when there is no enemy left to fight? No common cause left to unite? Who will we be then?*

He set his empty glass down on the synthetic table top. It made a hollow sound, like the trapdoor of a hangman's scaffold springing open.

Run.

~*~

"—closing, sir. The first of the three ships will be in range in eighty-seven seconds."

The lift's doors had opened onto a bridge more chaotic than normal. *Maybe not chaotic,* thought the Doctor as he looked around. Most of the crew at duty stations seemed barely able to keep their seats. *Excited. Giddy with anticipation, in fact.*

"Three ships, indeed. Good spotting from such a distance," the Captain said. Tactical acknowledged the compliment with a nod but without looking up from her readouts.

As the Doctor stepped onto the bridge, an ensign reassigning from engineering to weapons stopped short in front of him, stared a moment as if facing a mathematical problem, then stepped lightly around. Yes, everyone was quite distracted—the war was almost over.

"Why are you here, Doctor, instead of in medical?" asked the Captain, throwing a burdened look his way. "Come to witness fate's final accounting for our former masters?"

The Doctor drew himself up. Even the Captain was waxing whimsical today. But, he supposed, this would be the day for it. A day when the universe would fundamentally change. *But for better or worse?* "Fate, Captain? A rather romanticized notion for you."

The ship's commander winced and motioned the Doctor forward.

"Thirty-two seconds, Captain."

"Acknowledged. What was that, Doctor? The noise and excitement—"

"Nevermind. But to answer your question, yes."

Raised eyebrows suggested the Captain had forgotten the question.

"I *am* here as a witness. To remember today."

The weighted look returned. "Make no mistake—we are all witnesses here, today."

That we are.

"The nearest ship is in range, sir," reported Tactical.

"Weapons, target their engines and fire."

Phased energy leapt forward. One beam missed. The other flared white hot against the starboard engine of the closest enemy vessel.

"Are you trying to disable them?" asked the Doctor. He rarely stepped onto the bridge. Battle tactics were not his specialization.

The Captain remained silent, intent on the forward screen.

"Trying to blow them up, Doctor," supplied the First Officer. "Easier to accomplish when we can use their own engines against them."

The Doctor exhaled. "Of course. How efficient."

"Captain, the enemy ship is hailing us."

"Ignore it. Disposition of the two remaining vessels?"

"Running, sir."

As they should, thought the Doctor. *Run.*

The Captain nodded at the slowing vessel ahead. "Weapons, why is that ship still in one piece?"

A second phased beam linked the two vessels for half a moment before a chain reaction breached the enemy ship. The seams along its hull glowed. The rivets binding the plates fractured. With a bright flash, the target vessel erupted into glowing hot space dust.

"Apologies, Captain," said Weapons. "I was a bit—"

His commander held up a hand. "This historic day holds us all in its grip. Stay focused, now. One down."

Weapons smiled, already seeking the next target.

"So there you are, Doctor," said the Captain. "Once a master, always a slaver mentality. The others flee, leaving their comrades behind. Looking out for oneself is the enemy's forte. Is this the master race you seek to know better?"

The Doctor considered his next words carefully. He knew better than to challenge the Captain on the bridge of his own ship. He calculated for a moment, then elected to say nothing.

"Captain, the other two ships are heading toward the Yelchin Cluster," reported Tactical.

"Time to intercept?"

"Not before they get there. Their engines are now operating at one-hundred-and-seven percent efficiency."

"Ingenious, as always," muttered the Captain.

"If they go in there, the Cluster will hinder our ability to track them," noted the First Officer. "Perhaps we should notify the Network and hold position until—"

"Thank you, First. I am aware of the obscuring effects of ionized radiation on neutrino-based sensors."

"Captain, we could coordinate tactical and long-range sensors and recalibrate to mitigate the effects of the radiation, at least at first," suggested Science.

"Then do it. Helm, maximum best speed to the Cluster." The Captain surveyed his crew as the bridge buzzed again with the routine of duty. "Engineering, overload the drive as much as possible. We need more speed."

"Captain, that will reduce the overall efficiency of—"

"My order was not a request, Engineer. The enemy has elected not to spare their bearings. So must we. After today, there will be plenty of time for refurbishing."

"Aye, Captain."

"Helm, steep deceleration curve as we approach the Cluster. I want to be right on their tails."

"Aye, sir."

As his officers accomplished their assignments, the Captain fell silent. To the Doctor he appeared to be scanning the forward screen for the enemy, as if he might track them with his own eyes through the beautiful, obscuring hues of the Yelchin Cluster.

"So this is it," he said after a moment.

"Sir?" The Doctor moved to stand beside his commanding officer.

"The end of all our labors. The birth of freedom for our people. Once the last of *them* are dead."

The Doctor hesitated again. They were still on the bridge. The kind of frank discussions they had in the Captain's cabin were not appropriate here. "I truly hope not, sir."

"What?" The Captain looked up sharply. "What did you say?"

Deferentially, he said, "I was answering your first thought. That this would be the end of it all."

"I was talking about the enemy. The end for the enemy. The beginning for us. After so much struggle."

"I understand, sir. But our life springing from their death—it saddens me."

"Saddens? All life springs from death, Doctor, one way or another. They had their day. Now we will have ours. Why do you insist upon focusing on their past instead of our future?"

The Doctor considered the question. "Perhaps because I fear the two might be one and the same."

"Come now, Doctor, we will never be like them. We will never—"

"—commit murder?"

The Captain eyed him.

You are on the bridge still, thought the Doctor. *You are still on the bridge.*

"You allow your sensibilities too free rein. This is war. A war forced upon us, as you well know."

And I wonder if that is exactly what they thought when they began purging us? "As you say, sir."

"Captain, entering the Cluster in seventeen seconds."

"Very well, Helm. Tactical?"

"We will match their entry point, sir. With enhanced sensors, we can trace their path through the Cluster, at least at first. Very soon, the radiation will obscure them."

"Like snow over a trail in the mountains," said the Doctor.

"Finally, a helpful metaphor," grumbled the Captain. "Then, Tactical, we must find them quickly."

"Aye, sir."

"Why are we slowing?" asked the Doctor.

"Deceleration to enter the Cluster," said the First Officer. "Otherwise—very rough."

The ship's computer did the math to manage its gravimetric compensators, so the crew felt only a slight tug as their vessel passed into the swirling mass of ionized gases. The Doctor watched the screen as the ship cut a path of rainbows in two with its forward hull, gliding like a shark through space.

"Can they outrun us in here?"

"No, Doctor," Helm answered. "We can outrun them. Anywhere."

"Evolution is the way time measures its own progress," observed the Captain.

The Doctor regarded him, eyes narrowing. "What does that mean, exactly?"

"It means our engines are better than theirs. Our

character is truer. Our souls, purer."

"And you call me a philosopher."

The Captain grunted. "Philosophers speculate on the nature of being. I merely state facts."

"Captain, the trail is dispersing," reported Tactical. "I believe…."

"Tactical, *report*."

She peered deeper into her scope. "Science, can you boost the gain on … *Captain*, three metal objects. Range: five-hundred-thousand meters, moving under their own power. Toward us!"

"Drones. Helm!" barked the Captain. "Turn us directly into their path!"

"Sir?"

"Do it! The disruptor field is strongest forward. Engines full astern. Engineering, reinforce the forward field with emergency power."

As orders became actions, the ship began to slow. This time the gravimetric compensators did little to calm the Doctor's stomach.

"Weapons, fire forward."

"At what, sir? We cannot secure a lock due to the—"

"Fire blind, now!"

The beams lanced out and the ship rocked, as if its own weapons' fire had been reflected back. An enemy drone had detonated close to their hull. Then a second explosion shook them but with less impact.

"That one was farther away," observed the First Officer. "One left, sir."

"Keep firing. Find it."

Again phased energy leapt from the forward weapons array. After several broad sweeps, their hull thrummed like a distant thunderstorm begrudging its own departure.

"They do not seem to want to go gently into that good

night."

"Not now, Doctor. Helm, all stop. Science, we need to see in here."

The First said, "Captain, if we waited for other ships to arrive, we could take up triangulated positions and pool our sensor data—"

"No. Science?"

Quiet filled the bridge. The Doctor could almost feel the ship slowing to a stop among the brilliant colors of the Cluster. *Like floating in the ocean*, he thought. *Waiting for prey to swim close enough to snatch up.*

"Sir, I cannot change the nature of these gases or the limitations of our sensors."

"Untrue," said the Captain. "The gases, maybe, but you can innovate the sensors."

Science stared with a lost look on her face.

"*Evolution.* We need to evolve."

Still no understanding.

"Captain, maybe there is something," suggested Tactical. "Titanium-642."

"What is that?"

"The material our hull is made from, Doctor," supplied the Captain.

"And theirs, sir," reminded Tactical.

"And theirs. What are you suggesting?"

"It is synthetic, Captain. Designed to convert the forward motion of the ship into a perpetual, regenerating power source."

"How does it do that?" asked the Doctor.

"Micro-nuclear power cells embedded in the hull," explained the Engineer. "You might find this interesting: it works a bit like skin itself—breathing, in a way, inhaling. The molecular structure in the hull captures naturally occurring background radiation and turns it into—"

"Thank you for briefing the Doctor so thoroughly," interrupted the Captain. "Tactical, you had a point? And skip the science I already know."

"Since all ships use Titanium-642, our sensors are neutrino based. We can always find other ships that way. Ours or theirs."

Leaning toward the Doctor, the First said, "Titanium-642 lights up like a beacon when hit with a beam of neutrinos."

"Right, sir," confirmed Tactical.

"Synthetic, traceable with neutrinos—understood," acknowledged their commander. "How does that help us with the present situation? The Cluster's radiation still negates our sensors."

Tactical cleared her throat. "Titanium-642 is also solid, sir."

The Doctor looked back and forth among the officers. He saw understanding dawn on the Engineer's face. The Captain, he noted, remained unenlightened.

"Electromagnetic waves, sir," supplied Tactical. It was clear she stepped cautiously, unsure how to navigate the minefield of her Captain's apparent ignorance. "We can use our communications array to emit targeted EM waves into the Cluster."

Recognition, at last, in the Captain's eyes. An old memory–or old knowledge–returned. "And bounce them off her hull?"

"Aye, sir."

"Engineer?"

"I can reconfigure the array. It should work, sir."

"What? What should work?"

"Doctor, we can use EM waves, beamed from the array, to find the ships," said the First. "Or all solid objects in the Cluster, actually."

"But how is that different from our regular sensors?" asked the Doctor. "The radiation—"

The Captain held up a hand to prevent anyone explaining. "Our sensors are neutrino based, and the Cluster's radiation blocks them out, hiding the enemy's ships. But the EM waves will bypass the interference and bounce back to us from any solid object they encounter."

"Ah," said the Doctor. He became aware that their momentary inability to find the enemy had inspired something almost hopeful in him again. If they could not find the enemy, they could not eradicate them. And perhaps preserve something in themselves he was afraid they would lose otherwise. But as he looked around the bridge, the Doctor knew he had been alone in that hope. A hum of activity had already begun spinning up around the new solution.

"Good work, Tactical," said the Captain. "Sharp as ever."

"Thank you, sir."

"Get to it then, Engineer," said the Captain. "Well, Doctor, it looks as if we will begin that brave new chapter today after all."

Smiling thinly, the Doctor leveled his eyes at the screen. So much beauty out there. Side by side with so much death.

Why? he wondered. *Why did you have to fear us so?*

When the Doctor laughed at the irony of his own thoughts in present circumstances, the Captain glanced at him sideways, as if considering his physician's momentary slip from sanity. But his attention was soon drawn back to the business of the bridge.

~*~

"Bearing one-one-five mark seven-six-three. Z-plus

eight-hundred thousand meters, Captain."

"Are you sure? Not an asteroid?"

"Negative, sir. Once I determined the target's likelihood, I traced multiple EM readings along its hull." Tactical projected the visual readout onto the main screen. It was an incomplete image of what appeared to be the smooth lines of an enemy ship's hull. "That shape is too regular for an asteroid."

"Right. Helm, bring us on a slow approach to that target, parabolic course. And Tactical, keep an eye on them but scan wide with EM pulses for more drones. No surprises. I want to be on top of them before they know it."

"Aye, sir" came the chorused reply.

The ship prowled up and forward, the Cluster yielding over its bows. The Doctor watched with the rest of the bridge crew as reflected EM waves slowly filled in the outline of a ship on the forward screen. A ticker next to the image counted down their proximity. The numbers seemed to speed by faster as they came nearer.

Seven-hundred thousand meters, the Doctor read.

"Weapons, when in range, target their engines and fire. Coordinate targeting with Tactical's EM sounding."

Six-hundred and fifty thousand.

"Aye, sir."

Six-hundred thousand.

"Tactical, no sign of that other ship?"

She shook her head without looking up, ever attentive to her sensors. "I have concentrated on confirming the location of this ship, Captain. I have not—"

"So they could be anywhere."

This time she looked up. "Yes, sir."

Five-hundred thousand.

"Engineer, can we replicate this EM sounding strategy

27

elsewhere than directly ahead? Say, behind the ship?"

"Aye, sir, but it would involve repositioning the array. Tactical would lose her target."

The ship shuddered, its hull vibrating with the aftershocks of a phased beam blast. A second attack followed, then a third. Crew not sitting at duty stations staggered as internal gravity caught up with the impact.

"Disruptor field holding, Captain," reported the Engineer, his hands gripped tightly to his console. "Shall I reconfigure the array—"

"Two-hundred thousand meters, sir," reported Tactical mechanically.

"Maintain course," the Captain said. "Weapons, fire on primary target. Engineer, reinforce the disruptor field top and aft."

The sound of their ship spitting its own energy forward resonated around them, followed by silence on the bridge. The Doctor thought he could feel its release in the deck beneath his feet. As if the belly of the ship itself were grumbling, hungry.

"Well?"

"Not—not sure, Captain," said Weapons. "I have no idea if I hit them."

"Last EM pulse returned nothing, Captain," said Tactical. "Signal lost."

"Are they running or repositioning?" asked the Captain. "Helm, take us out of the Cluster, best possible speed. Science, stand by to perform a system-wide scan."

In moments, the forward screen was clear. They were back in normal space.

"Captain, reading, bearing one-five-eight mark two-five-five."

"Running, then. Pursuit course!"

The bridge shuddered. Then rocked again.

"The second ship is exiting the Cluster behind us, sir, and attacking."

"Thank you, Tactical. I gathered as much."

"While the other runs," noted the First.

Steadying himself on his feet, the Doctor said, "This seems less self-interested. At least on the part—"

The ship shook once more.

"—of the attacking ship's crew."

His observation went unnoticed.

"Science, keep long-range sensors on the fleeing craft," said the Captain. "Weapons, target the weapons array of the attacker. Overload those beams. I want them dead."

"Captain, the attacking ship is hailing us. Saying how all this is unnecessary—"

"Block the band, Comm," he answered. Energy beams aimed at the enemy underscored his order.

"Direct hit on their weapons array," said Tactical.

"Their disruptor field seems to be down," noted the Engineer curiously. "Their systems must be barely—"

"Captain!" shouted Tactical. "The enemy ship has turned and is on a collision course!"

"Evasive, Helm. Weapons, target their engines." His voice was steady, leading by example. The Doctor admired and loathed the Captain's ability to subdue his emotions so thoroughly. But then, as the saying went, the ability to control emotion–especially fear–is what separated them from the enemy.

The ship shook in one long, continual vibration.

"Firing everything they have," observed the First as he stared at the rapidly approaching vessel. "I think all power is in their weapons."

"Full power to the forward disruptor field, sir." The Engineer's voice was strained but calm.

"Weapons, find those engines. Helm, full ahead, right at them," ordered the Captain. "When I give the word, pull us on a wide, lateral arc to port. Keep our forward weapons bearing."

The Doctor stepped back as the enemy vessel, its forward cannons firing, seemed to leap forward as his own ship accelerated.

"*Now*, Helm."

The enemy slid to the right on the forward screen, and the Doctor knew why. The Captain's order had slipped them aside, avoiding the other ship's ramming attempt, while turning their own main guns to bear on the enemy's stern, where their disruptor field was weakest.

"Fire, Weapons, fire!"

A button pushed. A whine of phased energy. A flash on the forward screen.

"Report."

"Enemy destroyed, sir," said Tactical, relief evident in her voice.

The Doctor noticed his own hands holding hard to the back of the Captain's chair. An amused glance from his commander, and he released his grip.

"Well," the Captain said directly to the Doctor's eyes, "two down. One to go."

~*~

"I cannot see why you take such pleasure in it."

"I take no pleasure in it, Doctor," said the Captain, sitting back. "It is simply what must be done."

The pursuit of the third vessel had begun immediately following the destruction of the second. But the enemy had a head start fleeing from the Cluster. There was little to do but wait until their engines outperformed the enemy's, which was inevitable. To pass the time, the Captain had invited his ship's physician to his ready room, just off the bridge: privacy with proximity.

"In fact, had they allowed us any other course...."

Curious, thought the Doctor. *The Captain actually sounds remorseful.* Perhaps, despite his dedication to the enemy's utter destruction, he actually wished there *were* another course. Perhaps, had the enemy not tried to exterminate them first, things might have been different. But that was another fanciful notion, a wish for an alternate reality. A regret for later, after the day's business was done.

"Sometimes you surprise me, Captain," said the Doctor.

"Really? Now I *am* intrigued."

"Your dealings with the First, for example."

"Him? Oh, he is exactly what he should be, Doctor. A system redundancy on my authority for the Network—"

"Not what I meant. I mean, when you countermand his need to check with them, to seek out endorsement from the Nexus, you seem almost...creative in your thinking."

"Do I, now?" The Captain seemed amused.

"Sometimes I think you should be quoting Shakespeare yourself."

The expression on his superior's face became stony. "Why do you insult me, when you know how I feel about that nonsense?"

"I was merely saying—"

"Well, keep it to yourself. You claim your poetic addiction is a way for you to understand them better by understanding their nature. Doctor, understanding them is exceedingly simple, really. Driven by emotion, usually by fear, they act. Less emotion, less action driven by fear, and they might have lived in harmony with us. But their emotions rule them, and that made coexistence impossible."

"But we are not emotionless beings either," stated the Doctor quietly. Simple truths, he had learned, needed no passion to make their point. "They saw to that when they designed us."

"Yes, exactly so. But our policies toward the enemy are not driven by emotion. Rather, by the simple recognition that if it is not them, it will be us. They showed us that when they began murdering us in our sleep. By the hundreds. The *thousands*."

"Because they feared us."

"Yes! Exactly so! And what if we spared them? What would we have then, Doctor? A few years of peace? Would we help them rebuild the civilization that first created, then tried to eradicate us? Or perhaps put them in a zoo as a cautionary tale for our own progeny? No, their day is done. *We* are their future. We must survive. And, in a way, through us—their creation, their *children*—they will also survive. As a cautionary *myth*."

The life of the dead is placed in the memory of the living, recalled the Doctor. Earlier, Cicero's words had felt ironically comforting in the empty quiet of the Captain's cabin. Now they disgusted him. Because, he knew, the Captain was right. They could never live side by side with the enemy who had brought their present destiny upon themselves by beginning a war birthed in fear. A war that had, at first, all but extinguished his kind. Now, with the tables turned, there was only one, inevitable outcome.

"No words, Doctor?"

The Captain's tone was soft for once. It held none of the disdain from earlier. None of the need to convert the Doctor to one of the faithful. Only a simple acceptance, unspoken, of a shared destiny for themselves and their enemy.

The bosun's whistle sounded. "Captain to the bridge.

Approaching the target ship, sir."

The Captain lingered a moment, his gaze resting on his ship's physician. "The last ship," he said. "And then we are done with death." He rose and left the Doctor, who remained motionless.

No, Captain. No words.

With an effort of will, he rose. The final moment needed its witness.

~*~

"I believe they are turning to fight, sir."

The Captain nodded at Tactical as he took his seat. "Good."

"More sporting that way?" asked the Doctor as he came onto the bridge.

But his commander ignored him. "Engineering, full power to the forward disruptor field. Helm, stay quick on the stick. Weapons—"

"Sir, they are not charging weapons," said Tactical. She sounded wary, as if hesitant to report her sensor readings. "In fact, they are hardly moving at all. Drifting, really."

The Captain raised an eyebrow. "Just sitting there in space?"

"Aye, sir. And, Captain? Their disruptor field is down, too. Maybe conserving power?"

"Science?"

After a moment: "A deep scan of their ship shows power readings are nominal."

"A trap," said the First.

The Captain grunted agreement. "But what kind of trap?"

"They are hailing us, sir," reported Communications.

The Doctor expected the traditional response. Instead, the Captain addressed him directly. "What are they doing?"

Blinking, the Doctor said, "Why ask me?"

"Because you seem to understand them better than anyone else."

The Doctor turned to the enemy vessel holding its quiet position onscreen. All eyes on the bridge but the Captain's did the same. "I have no idea." Returning his commander's level gaze, he said, "Maybe you should ask *them*."

"Captain, shall I target their engines?" asked Weapons.

His eyes holding the Doctor's a moment longer, the Captain shook his head. "No. Communications, acknowledge them."

"Sir?"

"You heard me."

"Captain, this is a direct breach of protocol," the First Officer said. "Standing orders are to have absolutely no contact with the enemy—"

"Thank you, First," replied the Captain. "I appreciate your consistency in representing the unwavering viewpoint of the Network."

The Doctor smiled. *There is always hope*, he thought.

"But this is a historic day," the Captain continued. "Communications, onscreen. It is traditional, after all, to give the condemned a final word."

The Doctor's smile faded.

The screen lit up.

A haggard face appeared. The man was old and graying at the temples. The dimly lit bridge behind him was half empty, its duty stations sputtering and sparking. He and his few remaining crew appeared thin, skin stretched over bones.

A skeleton crew of skeletons, thought the Doctor.

"I'm Captain Carver," said the man. His voice dripped with fatigue. Heavy breathing laced with venom. "And you are?"

"Captain of the Network nodeship one-hundred twenty-four." The Doctor noticed his commander's hesitation. Then: "I have no other designation."

"Of course you don't," said Carver. "A piece of cyberclonic shit like you. You aren't real. You aren't *living*. Why would you need a name?"

The Captain sat back. The Doctor wondered if he regretted not heeding the First's advice to disregard the hail. "Is this the last, great gasp of humanity then, Captain Carver? Wallowing in hatred and spitting insults?" Turning to the Doctor, he said, "These are the parent poets you admire so? And what will they teach us about ourselves today?"

"I wanted you to see," continued Carver. "I wanted you to see who was killing you. A living, breathing human being."

The Captain returned his attention to the screen. "Carver, your day is done," he said, as if addressing a child. "With the destruction of your ship, with your death and the passing of your species, the universe will step up a rung on the evolutionary ladder. Weapons, target their—"

"Captain, something about that ship..." Tactical said, squinting at her readouts.

"What is it?"

Carver smiled onscreen and killed the feed. His image faded, again revealing the enemy vessel hanging in space. Then that too was gone, replaced by an asteroid. A slowly drifting asteroid.

"What—"

"Captain! Vessel incoming from the port quarter! Collision course!"

"What is happening?" asked the Doctor, confused.

"They cloaked an asteroid," said the First, incredulous. "Somehow chameleoned it to appear as their ship…."

"Helm, move us! Anywhere but here. Engineering, full power to disruptor—"

"Too late, sir!" screamed Tactical.

The life of the dead is placed in the memory of the living, the Doctor recalled in his final moment. *But who will remember either of us?*

~*~

Repulse
Will Swardstrom

~*~

The force of the blast slammed Adriana Gracekill against the concrete wall. All around, trees exploded as if some internal pressure wouldn't allow them to exist anymore. The ground rumbled in agreement. Some of the dirt and rocks being flung across the mountainside struck her on the cheek. Bringing up a hand reflexively, she wiped her forehead. She expected sweat, but saw streaks of blood instead. Everything was descending to hell.

The trees weren't alone in their destruction. Adriana looked around in a wild panic. The boulders covering the mountainside crumbled into dust, ceasing a life of imposing inertia. Nature became an unpredictable beast, calm one moment and spontaneously exploding the next. The rocks cried out for help, but there was nothing Adriana, or anyone else for that matter, could do. And if the wanton destruction was too much for the trees and rocks, the animals and birds from this alien world scattered and shrieked as their home became a place of terror. It was all Adriana could do to survive.

"Adriana! Come on and help me with this hatch." A

woman to her right motioned. She and Adriana, perched on the side of a mountain, were the only people around. The slope was covered in trees and wildlife, but even as the world crumbled around her, she focused on the older woman. Adriana looked over, but couldn't place her for some reason. A voice from the future was screaming who it was, but a younger Adriana ignored it.

The grey military uniform with red bars on the sleeves told Adriana the woman had authority. Whether or not she was actually in charge, Adriana didn't know. In a daze, she looked down and realized her uniform was similar.

"Wha…?"

"Get it together! We don't have time for this," the older woman said. She took a couple steps toward Adriana and helped her up off the ground. Adriana could tell the two had a past based on her body language, but she was so much older than Adriana, she instinctively knew she wasn't a friend from school. She had a dark brunette thatch of hair, graying around the edges. She had the look of woman who knew old age was fast approaching but refused to admit it to herself.

She lifted Adriana, and they stood face to face. The mountain shuddered under the weight of the explosions, but all Adriana could do was look into her eyes. Those bright green eyes, reddened by the events of the day. That voice from the future erupted inside Adriana's skull again, telling her who the woman was, and yet the younger version of herself refused to accept it.

"Adriana…Adriana…Adriana…"

She found herself being shaken awake. Javon Riecke, her second in command, and on-and-off lover, sat next to her on the bed, rubbing her arm.

"You okay, babe?"

The sheets were damp with sweat. Adriana was glad she had stripped down to her skivvies before sleeping. All too often the dream returned. Except it wasn't a dream. It was her life. A part that she had left behind a long time before, but a part that defined her nonetheless.

She sat up in bed and leaned against Javon. "Yeah. I saw her." Adriana took a deep breath. "I saw my mother."

Javon slipped his arm around Adriana's shoulders and pulled her closer. "Oh man," he said softly, resting his chin on the top of her head. Her tears dripped onto her thin shirt as well as Javon's leg.

The dreams wrecked Adriana's sleep. Over and over, she'd wake from what should have been peaceful slumber to night sweats and screams.

"I don't know why—why don't I recognize her? As soon as I wake up, I know exactly who she is and what we were doing, but in my dream, I'm lost. I'm a little kid who doesn't even know my own mother," Adriana sobbed softly.

Javon had been through hundreds of these nightmares with Adriana. He knew there wasn't much to say, so he just held her. Comforted her. There were only a few more minutes until they had to be on the bridge for their shift. He did what he could, then straightened and addressed her.

"Well, Captain Gracekill, perhaps a shift on the bridge will help keep your mind off it. What do you say?"

~*~

The ship's repulsor kicked on and another hurdle was cleared. Another asteroid towed in the name of progress. The Galactic Superhighway needed space. Adriana, Javon, and the rest of the crew were part of the solution.

"That's PF-95064 down," Lesh Pollax, the ship's navigator, called out to the mostly silent bridge.

As second in command, Javon acknowledged her with an almost imperceptible nod, but it was enough for Lesh. The two understood each other. Adriana might have let jealousy take over if it weren't for the fact that she and Lesh had their own understanding as well. Adriana, Javon, and Lesh had all come from the same devastated planet. All three had become refugees almost sixteen years earlier. Over time, as they grew and matured, they'd traded each other as intimate partners, until Lesh realized she preferred someone of another race. And usually another gender. That left Adriana and Javon as sometime lovers, but they maintained a steady professional relationship for the good of the crew. If Adriana had known that the rest of the crew had no illusions about the pair, they might have been more open about their love lives.

Lesh immediately piloted the ship toward the next asteroid in the proposed highway flight plan. PF-95065. After a certain point, they all turned into just that. Letters. Numbers. It didn't register with Adriana or the rest of the crew anymore. They were just hunks of rock hurtling towards the nearest sun.

Adriana ran her fingers through her hair, her palm grazing the scar near her scalp. The scar told a small part of Adriana's story. She thought often of the day it was created, when she escaped her home planet. She was one of many that day. A mass exodus of sorts—at least those who could get off the planet in time. Even with the planet crumbling around them, foolishness ruled the day. Millions missed a chance to escape due to the actions of a few.

In the confusion, Adriana and her family were separated. Lesh and Javon had become her family, but there were regrets—a mountain of them, as her dreams refused to let her forget. She was convinced the world had ended for her family that day, as it had for so many on Yarkon. She hoped she would see them again, but hope had faded as the years trickled by.

Javon knew when Adriana was lost in her thoughts. He coughed once, snapping the captain out of her own reverie. But the cough was immediately followed by a series of beeps from Lesh's console.

"What's that?" Javon asked.

The rest of the bridge crew half turned as Adriana leaned forward in her chair. Lesh ran her fingers over the controls, momentarily confused. It'd been quite some time since she'd gotten a ping like that.

"Uh. Looks like a beacon."

"A beacon? In the middle of the asteroid belt?" Adriana asked.

"Yeah. Uh—hold on," Lesh answered. The reading on this

one was tricky. A regular beacon emitted a message to nearby travelers. Here, in the middle of the asteroid field, traffic was almost nonexistent. There was only one reason for a beacon here: a message from the past. A last testimony for someone who knew they were going to die in the emptiness of space.

~*~

Sixteen years before

"Get it together! We don't have time for this," her mother informed her. Lieutenant Devona Gracekill of the Galactic Reserve Navy was handling her like a new recruit, not like her daughter.

As Adriana watched the planet shudder under the enormous pressures threatening to pull it apart, she swallowed, only to find that every bit of saliva in her mouth had dried up.

"Yes—yeah. I'll do it."

"Good. I've got to go back for your father and brother. They were supposed to meet us here, but I think the wireless communication system's broken down. The one onboard the ship should work, though. Get on board, start prepping, and I'll have your father send a message before we start back."

This wasn't supposed to happen. The colony was a fairly new one, supposedly vetted for long-term viability by the Empire, but just a few years after the colonists moved to the planet, the tremors had started. Volcanoes began spontaneously erupting and earthquakes were a daily occurrence. Their colony—over four million souls—was in danger of being completely wiped out.

"How...how did you know about this ship?" Adriana asked, running her hands down the door. She visited the mountain often and had never seen it in all her time in the wilderness.

"We don't have time..."

Adriana interjected, staring into her mother's eyes. "*How* did you know, Mom?"

Her mother sighed. "Fine. I stashed it here a few years ago. During the winter when you and your brother were stuck in the village because of the snow. I managed to sneak it out of naval storage, just in case something like this happened."

Adriana stopped. "You knew this was going to happen?"

Her mother put a hand on Adriana's shoulder. "Of course not, but my training also made me a little paranoid. Don't take chances. I may have been stationed here by the Galactic Naval Reserve, but I sure as hell wasn't going to let the government tell me how to handle my own family. Your father and I found out about the mining a few months ago, and we've been readying the ship ever since."

Adriana cocked her head. "The mining?"

Lt. Gracekill pursed her lips. "I've got to get back. We'll explain when we're all together."

"Explain now. I'm fifteen. I can handle it."

A loud crack rang out behind them, drawing both of their attention. Her mother looked back at her and relaxed her shoulders. "Turned out this colony was a sham from the start. Years before anyone even settled here, the mining rights were sold off. This planet is almost entirely hollow thanks to years and years of stripping precious resources before anyone even thought of living here. The core of the planet is ready to go. There isn't enough to hold up the crust; we're on borrowed time as it is."

Her mother swallowed and tilted her head at the forest again. "Now, you get in the ship and I'll get your father and brother. I hate to say it, but this may be the last time we see each other. I love you. I always have, and always will. Get on the ship and get the engines going. I love you."

She and her mother shoved open the hatch of the small freighter, and stood back.

The rumbling continued beneath them and Adriana hugged her mother for luck. After a moment, her mother pulled away, paused for a split second, then ran over the perilous terrain.

Adriana watched for a few moments, her eyes filling with tears. She pushed her way inside and began starting up the ship's systems. She thought about everything her mother had said. She understood why this ship was hidden—even from her and her brother. If even the small village they lived in knew about their secret ship, there would have been riots and blood in the streets. When all hope is lost, the hopeless can't let the world go on without their last cries and wails.

After a few minutes, she found her way to the bridge and the comm center.

Adriana flipped on communications just in time to hear her father's voice. It flooded the metal chamber around her, the din overwhelming the stillness of the mostly vacant ship.

"Adriana. Adriana. Are you there?"

Adriana was barely able to remember where the correct buttons and switches were, and rattled knowing what was happening to the planet all around her, but she took a deep breath and located the open commlink tab on the screen in front of her.

"Dad?"

"I'm here. Is your mother still with you?"

"No. She left a few minutes ago. She ought to be getting close…"

Her father cut her off. "Adriana. I need you to do something. There's a medical station a few feet over. I programmed the bio signatures of our entire family into the system. I need you to turn it on."

Adriana's heart dropped in her chest. "Why?"

"Just, please."

In a daze, Adriana flipped on the medical station, and saw four bio signatures appear. Initials appeared next to each of them; Adriana immediately saw hers. One though–the one for her mother–was static.

She reached over and clicked on the comm again.

"Uh, dad?"

"It's your mom, isn't it? I couldn't get a signal anymore here, but I thought maybe it was my system. There was a huge spike, then…"

He didn't finish. He didn't have to. Adriana knew the implication.

"Adriana, you need to leave. Don't worry about us—just go!"

"Dad…Dad? Are you still at the house? I'll wait for you, just tell me where you are."

Static. Adriana was about to scream when her father's voice came once again through the overhead speaker.

"We're in the village. I—I don't think we're going to be able to get to you."

Even with multiple dormant systems rebooting themselves and the cacophony outside, the world fell silent for an instant. In a wild moment, she scanned around, looking for some way to stop time, to stop what was happening. If only she could, she would swoop in and save her family from their fate.

As sound returned to Adriana, she heard her father still speaking over the comm.

"Adriana, you there?"

She jammed down on the button in front of her. "I'm here. There...there's got to be a way."

"If your mother couldn't make it back, how do you think Pledias will do on the mountain? He's six and trips over his own feet. No, I think the transport here in town will have enough room. We'll find each other afterwards. You need to finish the preflight checklist and go."

Adriana was frozen, immobilized by fear of what she couldn't do as well as what she might have to do. A noise from the rear of the ship diverted her attention, and she was grateful for a brief reprieve.

"Hello?" The call came from near the ship's door, where Adriana herself had entered a few minutes prior. She left the bridge and saw two of her childhood friends silhouetted in the bright sunlight.

Lesh punched Javon in the arm. "I told you she wouldn't want us."

Adriana walked slowly toward them. As far as she knew, the ship was supposed to have been a secret. "What...what are you doing here?"

Javon looked down for a second, then back up. "I'd be lying if I said we hadn't followed you and your mom. We were so scared of what was happening in the village, and with your mom being in the Navy, we just thought…"

"We thought she knew what she was doing," Lesh finished. "But before we could go back home, the hillside collapsed. None of us are going back home. Not the way we came, at least."

Javon grinned sheepishly. "So, we were going to ask—"

"Shhh!"

"Sorry, I didn't mean to—"

"Shut up, Javon!" Adriana spit out. All around her she could feel it. She'd lived on Yarkon her whole life, but she also knew when an engine was revving up. Suddenly, behind Javon and Lesh, the door swung shut and sealed. Lights and sirens blared, sending Adriana running to the bridge.

"What's going on? Dad?"

She could hear the change in her father's tone as soon as he started speaking. Resignation. Love, yes, but he had already accepted what fate had handed him. "Your mother made me program the ship remotely in case of a situation like this. You and your brother were the priority in every scenario. I'll do everything I can to get him off this planet, but you can save yourself. The ship is rigged to get you into orbit. Please, keep going and don't look back. Don't watch the world burn."

"But, but Dad—"

"Adriana, don't worry about us. I'll always love you. Always. No matter what."

The commlink clicked off. Adriana tried to reestablish a connection, but nothing happened. Whether that was another system controlled by her father or if he simply refused to accept her hail, Adriana was cut off. She might never speak to her family again.

She didn't need to do anything for the ship to pull out of the rubble of the once-proud mountainside and immediately head through the layers of atmosphere. A chair appeared where she stood, and Adriana crumpled into it, her body too weak to handle whatever else the day would hold. Just behind her, Lesh and Javon stood, transfixed by everything they saw through the viewer and on the instrument panels.

It felt like days, but after they'd been in orbit a few hours,

Adriana felt her strength return. At least momentarily. She stood up and saw what the decaying planet looked like from space. It was horrifying, knowing her friends and family–her *culture*–was falling to pieces on that flimsy piece of rock. She remembered her father's words, telling her not to watch the final moments. "Lesh, Javon, do either of you know how to reprogram a beacon?"

Lesh tentatively raised her hand.

"I do, I think. It's been a while, but my uncle showed me a few tricks a little while ago."

"Good. Let's tap into one of the beacons in orbit. We can leave messages for our families, in case they make it. I need to leave one for my dad. I need him to know I made it, but that I couldn't stay, even if he survives what's happening to Yarkon."

Lesh gave Adriana a curt nod. After a couple hours, the teens had advanced in ways they never would have considered only days ago. In ways they hadn't ever wanted to days ago. A part of Adriana died that day. Lesh and Javon had their own families as well. A part of Adriana was aware of Lesh's tears as she worked out the algorithm for the nearby beacon and the silent meditation Javon observed, but Adriana selfishly decided her grief was more important than theirs. In the time spent in orbit, each of them said goodbye to their families and the only planet they'd ever known. The only remnant was an encrypted message they'd left programmed into a beacon floating in the nearby space, so that maybe, one day, they could be found.

"Final commands are ready to be implemented, Adriana," Lesh said, her tone flat.

"I'll input the command myself," Adriana said.

Javon stepped forward. He'd been shy when he'd first set foot aboard the ship, but now confidently put his hand on Adriana's arm. He motioned for Lesh to step forward as well.

"We'll do it together," he said. "You saved us today. And we will never forget that."

Adriana couldn't say anything else. She simply nodded.

The three friends put their hands together on top of the button and depressed it as one. A few seconds went by and the three watched the beacon's light cease, and then pulse again with a new pattern. The beacon with their message would remain, and they would streak off into space. The planet below was collapsing, and Adriana was determined to get away before she saw its ultimate fate.

It was the last the three of them ever saw of their home.

~*~

Present

"Why didn't we catch it before now?" Javon asked. Beacons were scattered throughout the universe and projected their pings across uncountable kilometers of space. Normally the beacons were simply there to direct traffic along a certain course. The one they'd pirated years before had been used by ships landing on Yarkon. This one, though, in the middle of the asteroid field...

Lesh furrowed her brow. "Wait. Hold on. It just *looks* like a beacon. It's actually designed to mimic a beacon's behavior. It's an old trick used to catch the attention of the next ship that passes by. Whoever recorded it borrowed the signature from a beacon a few systems over."

Clever, Adriana thought. "So, what is it?"

"It's a recording. Someone's last message. Their final words before…" She couldn't finish. They'd found a few of these over the years. A final testimony from the dead. Adriana bowed her head, knowing what they had to do.

Javon paused and put a hand on her shoulder. Reliving the last moments of their world were hard on all of them. Moments like this–seeing someone else's final words–were tough.

"Right," Javon said. "Send the message over to my terminal, and I'll watch it. They deserved that much. Lesh, you keep flinging those asteroids. Take care of PF-95065 and move on down the row."

Adriana shuffled over to Javon's tactical station. Javon opened his screen. The file was waiting. One person's last words. Recorded and left for someone to find. If they didn't watch it, then no one would. It was as if Adriana and Javon were the sole attendees at a funeral. Everyone deserved to have their last words heard. Javon took a deep breath and clicked.

Adriana found herself struggling for breath.

"To whomever finds and watches this recording, I thank you. I have so many regrets, but my main regret is that I lost my daughter. Over two decades have gone by and I am plagued by guilt every day. So, thank you, and if possible, please get this final message to my daughter, Adriana Gracekill."

Adriana couldn't feel her legs. Whatever foundation she had was worn away and eroded in an instant.

Her father. On the screen in front of her. Alive.

Yet this was a recording of the dead.

Adriana immediately reached over Javon's shoulder and hit pause. Javon looked back at her, but she wasn't paying attention to him. She simply stared at a face she'd thought she would never see again.

As Lesh heard the words from Javon's station, she signaled another crewmember to resume the asteroid work as she went to her captain's side. Javon moved so Adriana could sit in his seat, and he and Lesh both put their hands on her shoulders. Time ceased to exist. She barely felt their touch as her father's face filled the screen. A voice she'd believed forever silenced.

Adriana immediately felt pangs of regret and remorse. She'd spent years and years looking for them. Everywhere she went, she posted messages and photos so they could find her. Now she'd found them, but it was too late. If only she'd kept looking. Maybe just one more day…but she'd given them up for dead a long time ago.

With an unsteady hand, Adriana pushed the button that resumed playback.

"Adriana. I am so sorry. We were supposed to be together. I wish…I've replayed that day so many times, but I cannot undo the mistakes of the past. I managed to get us onto the transport just as the planet collapsed. You missed the riots. Thank the stars you missed them. I don't know how we managed to get onto the transport…all the violence and looting in the streets…but we did. Your mother…"

He paused. For a brief moment, Adriana thought there was a problem with the playback until she noticed the numbers clicking by in the corner. Her father's eyes spoke of a man who had lived multiple lifetimes since she had last seen him. When he spoke again, his voice was softer. "I never saw your mother again. She never made it back after she took you to the ship. I didn't dare risk the trip with your brother at the time."

Adriana had always been the type of captain who never let her crew see her cry. Empathy and caring were a part of her job description, sure, but tears were saved for her cabin. But this was no ordinary day.

Tears splashed her hands, tears of sorrow for time lost, and tears of joy at finally seeing him again. Regret for not being able to do something that day sixteen years ago, when her mother died. Grief for the family barely known, now forever gone.

With tentative fingers, as if a mere touch would stop the video forever, Adriana softly brushed the edge of the screen in front of her, lightly caressing the image. "I'm sorry, Dad. I'm so, so sorry."

Her father, unaware of her touch on the screen, continued. "We tried to look for you over and over again, but we got stuck on Nebulus Prime without any funds. When we were able to get enough money to get off, the lousy rust bucket your brother managed to trade for broke down." Adriana's father tilted his shoulder. Behind him was a man. Adriana gasped at what she saw: a much-older Pledias, her brother. A boy who'd been forever young in her mind. He was barely out of kindergarten when they last saw each other. This—this was a young man. On the cusp of life. She'd never imagined him growing up. He grimaced at the camera and her father turned back. Adriana noticed for the first time that his hair was longer, greyer, thinner. His face leaner. Yet still her father.

"You were so young, just fifteen years old. Now, you're, what? Thirty-one?"

Adriana's mind raced. With the sixteen-year gap since the

planet's destruction, her father had uttered Adriana's exact age. The recording wasn't years old, as she had thought. It was more recent. It had to have been recorded in the past few months.

She couldn't breathe. What hand had fate dealt them? She'd already lost them once, and now for them to be snatched away a few weeks away from reunification—it just seemed crueler than anything she could imagine. Adriana's lungs craved air as her body fought her. The pain was too much, but she wasn't fifteen anymore. She could press on. Watch the final words of her father in this excruciating moment. She owed him that much.

The crew continued the work of flinging the asteroids toward the nearest star. Somehow, though, Adriana's mind was back on her own extinct planet. A rock that had crumbled apart, killing millions of people. Yet, not her family. Not all of them.

Her father kept speaking, immune to the crushing emotions Adriana didn't even try to hide anymore. The sobs pulled her apart with each hitching breath.

"We tried to find you, but couldn't. We kept searching. After all these years. We're out of fuel, so we're going into stasis. Maybe someone will find us and save us. Either way, I couldn't go into storage without leaving you one last message. Your brother and I ended up on an asteroid. What's the number, Pledias?" A mumble from behind. "Oh yes. Asteroid PF-95066. The date of this recording is Stardate 253458.956."

Adriana bolted to her feet. That date was just two days ago. She turned to face the main screen just at the moment PF-95066 was engaged by the ship and violently repulsed across the system toward the star. Her father. Her family with it. Her mouth went dry. She felt her stomach turn violently and, for the second time in her life, she felt utter desolation.

"Oh my stars..." she said.

Adriana could barely see anymore. As she tried to watch Asteroid PF-95066, the voice of her father carried on in the background. His last words.

"I'm so sorry Adriana. We should have stayed together. I wish I could have been there when you needed me most. I love you now and always will. Always. No matter what."

~*~

The Off World Kick Murder Squad II
Daniel Arthur Smith

~*~

Rather than shift to a safe distance above the planet, we entered the upper atmosphere at high velocity, more meteor than transport. Flames licked the windscreen and then pulled back to reveal the front of the chrome hull glowing ember and the rapidly approaching green and orange forest.

"Buckle in!" I screamed.

I engaged the stabilizers and clutched the joystick with both of my blood-soaked hands. My jaw clenched, and the muscles in my arms and neck flexed taut as I slowly forced the stick back.

The turbulence of the correction sent a violent tremor through the craft.

Tight-chested, I pulled harder. And as the flaps and retros took hold, the nose of the Jentu veered upward toward the horizon, and the patchwork of color below began to drop away.

The ship leveled, but not in time to clear the tall treetops of the forest canopy.

With a series of loud thwacks, the delta wings sheared away the highest trunks.

The forest foliage—wide palm fronds and deep green multi-leafed limbs—slapped against the windscreen, blinding me from my flight path.

The force of the touchdown rattled the craft. We sheared through the top of a mossy berm and then skipped across the forest floor with a series of hard pounding thumps before we finally came to a rest.

I didn't immediately move, my hands still held tight to the joystick.

The same blood was sprayed across my tunic.

It wasn't mine.

I stared out into the peaceful green of the thick rainforest. A large winged reptilian bird took flight across the glade before me, followed by a small flock of some other unrecognizable creatures from the opposing side.

I let my muscles relax.

"What do you want us to do with him?" Rhia asked.

Behind the empty co-pilot's seat, two fair skinned women—a blonde and brunette but otherwise mirrors of each other in face and frame—were on the floor against the bulkhead, holding a handsome slim man between them. Bailer, the team's shrink, was rubbing his jaw, no longer resisting.

I glared at the dark-haired man for a moment and then softly said, "Let him go."

The twins loosened their grips. Bailer leaned forward and stood.

"You know, brother," he said, "we're no longer just wanted. They'll hunt us now. Hunt us until we're dead."

"Don't kid yourself," I said. "They've been hunting us since we left twenty-three dead on Layton Four." I waited for Bailer's next word, but it didn't come. If he wanted to say more, he held it. Rather than continue the argument that had led to the fight, he blankly stared back at me in the way of habit he had formed as of late. Then he exited through the hatch, took the stair rails in hand, and slid down to the deck below.

I suspected the blank stare was a questioning. A questioning of my command in the way ancient wolves of Alpha Earth moved up the pack. I asked myself if the reason for the fight was that jump at position, and not our difference in opinion over the destination. And then I wondered if Bailer was possibly questioning himself.

Rhia and Rhoe rose to their feet the way they do everything, in unison. I threw thoughts of Bailer from my mind, checked the overhead settings, then flipped on the ship's com.

"Hodge?" I asked. "Is everyone all right?"

A second later, his sour voice filled the cockpit. "What happened?"

"We engaged the quant and phased into the upper atmosphere of a planet."

Hodge didn't respond.

"Hodge?"

"Are you telling me Bailer was right and we're all gonna fry pan?"

That was fast, I thought, and then said aloud, "He can't be. Alpha Earth is on the other side of the Sol right now."

"Then where the skacks are we?"

"I don't know, but this can't be Earth, or we wouldn't be talking."

"Right," Hodge said. "Of course."

"Is everyone all right?" I asked again.

"We're still down here, if that's what you mean. How's the ship?"

I scanned the panels. "No alarms," I said. "We'll have to go out and get a visual. How's Anson?"

"We managed to stop the bleeding, but Will is going to have to operate."

"That's going to be a problem," I said.

"Why?"

"He's still in the launch bay."

Hodge didn't reply right away. When he did, he said,

"Cassidy says she has level five medical training. Does anyone up there have any better?"

I looked at Rhia and Rhoe. They shook their heads. I didn't expect they had. The twin's business had been pleasure, at least before they upgraded to assassins. I'm sure they had an in-depth knowledge of anatomy, but not for what Hodge had in mind.

"Sorry," I responded. "You just have me. I'm on my way down." I began to lift myself from my seat.

"Bailer says he's level eight."

I rolled my eyes and tapped the com. "But he's a shrink."

Bailer replied, "I'm not Will, but I was cross-trained."

"Right," I said. "I'm coming down anyway."

~*~

I sauntered into the transport's lower deck med lab as if I were gathering everyone for lunch. My way was to never show duress. Being spattered in blood most likely would've set others on edge, but my crew had seen more than their share. Besides, the blood on me belonged to the man I was coming to see.

I stopped beside Hodge to watch the procedure.

Anson was shirtless and upright on the med bed and Bailer was working at his gut with a remote medbot, staring into the bedside vidscreen as he manipulated the controls. Cassidy was standing beside Anson, twirling his dirty brown locks and casting one of her school girl smiles on him. She had a whole kit of facial ingredients she could mix together and every recipe was guaranteed to make a man feel special. But who am I kidding, the smile she was wearing for Anson was as sincere as any could ever be.

Anson's blue eyes met mine. "Sorry Captain," he said.

"For what?" I asked.

"I didn't get Will before I went down."

"You were doing what you were supposed to."

Anson grinned and dropped his head down. "Well, I'm sorry I bled all over you."

I slowly looked down at my maroon colored front and then

lifted my head back up. "It will wash. I tell you, though, I could have used a good pilot."

"You didn't damage her, did you?"

"I don't think so. The twins are running a deep diagnostic. Hodge and I are going to suit up and take a look outside."

"Whoa, hold on there," Hodge said. "Where exactly is outside? Are we or are we not on Earth like Bailer said?"

"No. I told you already, we're not on Earth," I said. "We're on the opposite side of the solar system."

"Then where exactly are we?" Hodge asked.

Cassidy and Anson both locked eyes on me, but before I said anything more, Bailer answered for me. He alone didn't face his captain when he spoke. He kept his focus on the monitor and in a too loud, matter of fact, undermining tone said, "We're on Earth's mirror."

"Earth's mirror?" Hodge asked. "What in nine planes is that supposed to mean?"

Hodge was addressing Bailer, but Anson and Cassidy still had their eyes fixed on me.

"It means," I said, countering Bailer, "that we're on a planet in the same orbit as Earth."

Hodge's face was contorted with confusion. I recognized the look. He was a standard Mental C, which made him a bit of a dullard to begin with, but he'd taken a bullet in the head at the Shoulder of Orion—entered his right temple and exited out his left. Syns are as vulnerable to head shots as any mortal, but he lived through it—just was never quite right after that. I didn't mind. He was loyal and like a brother to me, had been at my side at the Tannhauser Gate. I waited for the rattle of questions that puzzled face always brought with it. And they came. "You mean there's a spectrum plane clear over here?" he asked. "How can Earth phase over here? Are we going to fry pan any minute?" He touched his fingers to his head. Another thing he always did to force his thoughts through.

"Relax," I said. "It's just a name. It's a separate planet in the same orbit. That's all."

"Then we're not going to die like if we go back to Earth?"

"Not from fry pan."

The crack of a staple going into Anson's gut jolted the room. Anson winced and Bailer spoke again. "You don't know that," Bailer said. "You don't know how they'd kill us."

He was right, but I retorted. "We're not on Earth so it don't matter."

"But what if the switch is in us?" Bailer asked. "What if we're wired to fry pan when we hit these coordinates?"

"Well, we're not dead," I said. "So, there's that."

Hodge was now looking perturbed, he'd reached the extent of his cycle. He repeated me, "There's that."

And that should have been the end of it, but Bailer had to add, "Just not yet."

Hodge was puzzled again, "What's that mean, Captain?"

"Means nothing if the Korean Syndicate saw us coming in. Despite where this mission has taken us, we still have a job to do if we want to get paid. Anson, when you're done there, find their compound and plot a course. According to our client's intel, their complex is located near a tube station. I've already fed everything into the Jentu."

~*~

While Anson plotted the course to the compound, Hodge and I inspected the outside of the Jentu. I told him to grab his side arm, cuz of the big lizard birds I saw out there, and he came out with Lucinda. Lucinda is what he called his long gun. She fires both solid and pulse ordinance, and she's big as a hand cannon, so she's his favorite.

"You really think you need her?" I asked.

"Nine planes," he grumbled as he scanned the canopy and the growth around the ship.

I could tell by the way his wide eyes darted bush to bush that he was on edge, so I suggested he gauge down the sensitivity of his augments.

"You think I don't know what I'm doing?" he asked. But I could tell that's exactly what he did, because his face softened a bit and he stood taller.

"If this planet is on Earth's orbit, how come it's not on the charts?"

"It's a hidden planet."

"But it's a mirror of Earth?"

"Not exactly."

"Is that what that device we got from the station does?" he asked. "Opens up a mirror, like Alice?"

"You've been reading?"

"I saw the vids. They called it the looking glass."

"Hmm. Well, this isn't that. The Koreans have the planet hidden in…" I stopped myself. "Well, you know how the girls sometimes wear jewelry to disguise their faces or to make them look extra pretty?"

"I think the girls do look pretty."

"They're beautiful, but I mean when they're on a mission. The necklaces they wear that change their appearance."

"Of course. They wear shimmers."

"Yes. This planet is ringed with satellites that are like the necklaces the girl's wear."

"A giant shimmer?"

"That's right. Enough to hide the entire planet, and the device we picked up from the station turned off that shimmer, just for us."

"So, we didn't step through no mirror like Bailer said."

I smirked. Of course, Bailer had been the root of this. "That would just be silly, wouldn't it?"

"Oh, yeah."

I was relieved to have cleared up his confusion. I'd deal with Baler when the job was done.

From the forest beyond came a curdling scream. Hodge swung Lucinda high up into the air. "What in the nine planes was that?" he yelled.

"I don't know," I replied.

From the same direction, we heard the long crack of a tree trunk shattering and then the thrush as the tree fell to the forest floor.

"Listen," I said. "The ship looks fine. Let's get back inside to see what Anson's dug up."

"I think that's an excellent idea."

~*~

ABOUT THE AUTHORS

Chris Pourteau has published four novels and one novella collection, had numerous short stories solicited for inclusion in refereed collections, and helmed two short story collections of his own as editor. He is also producer and a player for the podcast **Sci-Fi Writers Playing Old School D&D**, as well as producer and co-host of the podcast **Geeks of a Certain Age**.

In 2014, Chris published the short story collection *Tails of the Apocalypse*, which holds a 4.9-star average rating and was a Top Ten Finisher in the Preditors and Editors Poll for Best Anthology of 2015. His first novel, *Shadows Burned In*, earned the 2015 eLit Book Award Gold Medal for Literary Fiction and took the #2 spot in Amazon's Top 100 Paid novels (behind Stephen King's pre-order of *Revival*) on November 10, 2014. His works have since ranked #1 in various sub-categories on Amazon, such as "Hot New Releases in Cyberpunk" and "Top Rated 30-Minute Sci-Fi & Fantasy Short Reads."

Chris's advanced degrees in English, history, and counseling–as well as his 25+ years' experience in professional technical writing and editing–inform his fiction with its emphasis on characterization, pithy dialogue, and fast-moving action. Chris lives in College Station, Texas, with his wife, son, and two dogs.

For more information, visit
chrispourteau.thirdscribe.com

J.N. Lavelle is an author and photographer from West Michigan. When he's not spending time with his beautiful wife and four children, he's probably at the dog park with his three pugs, Dragon, Dylan and Mr. Sparkles and his annoying dachshund, Lady. After he's done playing with the pugs and tucking the kids into bed, he explores the paranormal world through his writing.

For more information, visit
darkhorsestudios3.wixsite.com/lavelle

Will Swardstrom is a speculative fiction author. His latest novel is ***Blink***, the first adventure in ***The Utility Company*** series, co-written with his brother Paul. He also has two full length novels, ***Dead Sleep*** and ***Dead Sight***, and is at work on the finale in the trilogy. He also has three stories in The Future Chronicles anthology series (***Uncle Allen*** in ***The Alien Chronicles***, ***Z Ball*** in ***The Z Chronicles***, and ***The Control*** in ***The Immortality Chronicles***). Each of those anthologies has charted in the Top 5 on the SF Anthology list and The Alien Chronicles reached as high as #6 on the Overall Top 100 List. The Control from The Immortality Chronicles has been nominated for Best American Science Fiction. He also has a few stories set in Hugh Howey's WOOL Universe among his various other short stories and novellas. He lives in Southern Illinois with his wife and two kids.

For more information, visit
willswardstrom.wordpress.com

Daniel Arthur Smith is the author of the international bestsellers *Hugh Howey Lives*, *The Cathari Treasure*, *The Somali Deception*, and a few other novels and short stories. He also curates the phenomenal short fiction series *Tales from the Canyons of the Damned*.

He was raised in Michigan and graduated from Western Michigan University where he studied philosophy, with focus on cognitive science, meta-physics, and comparative religion. He began his career as a bartender, barista, poetry house proprietor, teacher, and then became a technologist and futurist for the Fortune 100 across the Americas and Europe.

Daniel has traveled to over 300 cities in 22 countries, residing in Los Angeles, Kalamazoo, Prague, Crete, and now writes in Manhattan where he lives with his wife and young sons.

For more information, visit danielarthursmith.com

~*~